The Illawarry Cassary

by **Pam Harvey**

illustrated by **Greg Gaul**

The Characters

Emu Flake

Martin Angus Alex

The Setting

CONTENTS

Dad and his mirrors

My dad is an antiques dealer. That means he goes around looking at old and rotting bits of furniture and buys them for next to nothing. He spends days and days fixing them up and then sells them so we can eat.

He specialises in mirrors. The workshop at the back of the house, where all this fixing up is done, has one whole wall of mirrors.

Some need frames, some are cracked, some need more black stuff on their backs, but Dad loves them all.

He polishes them with Mum's old tights and I reckon he talks to the mirrors as he does it.

I hate those mirrors. They're the reason I've got Emu and not a fifty kilogram dog that can bare its teeth and make your hair stand on end.

"Emu is clean, neat and won't wet the legs of my antique tables, if you know what I mean," said Dad.

He said this when I complained that other kids didn't have a chicken as their only faithful companion.

Emu isn't an ordinary chicken. He's a silky bantam. Silky bantams look a bit like they've got frayed cotton balls stuck all over them, especially on the tops of their heads.

Their head feathers shoot out like umbrellas over their faces. Silky bantam roosters have a grating, enormously loud COCKADOODLEDOO. But somehow it's not very scary when it comes out of a bird hardly bigger than a pigeon.

I have an Illawarry Cassary

Last Monday, at school, we were talking about our pets.

"Arnold is my rottweiler," said Angus McLean, who looks as though he eats whole cows for dinner. "He's been known to munch cats by the dozen."

"I've got a python called Sly," said Alex Browning, rubbing his football hands together. "He eats live rats."

"In an old fish tank at my place," said Martin Tan, "I've collected twenty-seven black widow spiders."

We all shuddered a bit at that one.

Then Angus said to me, "What sort of pet have you got at home, Flake?"

They call me 'Flake' because one day, just one day in my whole life, I had two bits of dandruff on my jumper. They might not have even been mine, but I've been stuck with Flake ever since.

And if you get called Flake, you aren't going to admit to owning a fluffy white chicken.

"I've got an illawarry cassary."

Angus eyeballed me. "A what?"

"An illawarry cassary. It's a type of meat-eating bird." I shrugged, acting really cool. "Dad found it on one of his antique runs. Its owner had died. Dad was buying up some old wardrobes when he saw this bird in a giant cage."

"Of course, he didn't know then it was an illawarry cassary or he wouldn't have brought it home." I sighed, trying to look as if it was too much to talk about. "He didn't realise it ate fox terriers."

"Get out of here!" Angus had crossed his arms over his chest. "You're bluffing, Flake."

I looked him in the eyes. "It's absolutely true."

"Didn't I ever tell you about the time it got out of its cage and flew over the fence? It ate Mrs Jeffers's poodle and flew back into our place with curly hair stuck in its claws. It kept spitting fur balls all over the lawn. That's how I caught it — it was choking on a big fur ball and I pushed it back into its cage."

Everyone was laughing, but they weren't sure. They were trying to work out if I was making it all up. Martin was even looking a bit sick (his mother owned a fox terrier).

"How come," said Angus, still standing with his elbows across his chest, "we haven't heard about this bird before?"

"You never asked," I said, and yawned as if I was really bored.

"Well, I'd like to see it."

I almost choked in mid-yawn. "You idiot!" I was thinking. Of course they'd want to see it.

I thought fast. "It always spits on strangers."

Angus shrugged.

"And some books say that it has a type of acid for saliva," I said.

Angus shrugged again.

"And it makes the most terrible noise. It can make you deaf with just one cry. We have to wear earmuffs all the time around the house in case it even cheeps."

Angus bent down to where I was sitting. I felt his breath, stinking of Marmite sandwiches, on my face. "I'm coming around tonight to see this illawarracrakaty. And so are the rest of us. Right, everyone?"

Everyone nodded, grins on their faces.

I gulped. "It's not an illawarracrakaty, it's an illawarry cassary," I managed to whisper.

"See you at five o'clock." They all walked off, leaving me feeling really stupid. What was I going to do now?

Plan C

I thought of three plans:

a) Becoming ill during Maths, so they'd have to cart me off to hospital. (Mr James would never believe me.)

b) Faking a robbery at our place. (How do you do that?)

c) Sticking pretend fangs onto Emu to make him look scary.

Plan C was the only one I could try.

Angus waved to me at the gate. "See you at five o'clock," he shouted.

He had to shout, not only because he had a loud mouth, but because dark clouds were rolling in across the sky. Booms of thunder drowned out anyone talking.

I ran home and got there just as rain, like falling icicles, came pelting down. There was a note on the table from Mum:

"Dad and I have gone to buy sandpaper and wood polish. Help yourself to biscuits."

"Great," I thought. Now I couldn't even get Mum to ring Angus's mum to tell her I had suddenly come down with a highly infectious disease. (That had been Plan D. I'd thought of it on the way home.)

It looked like I had to stick with the false teeth plan, so I cut triangles out of old butter containers and put tiny pieces of sticky tape on them.

Then I went down the stairs, through Dad's workshop and opened the doors to look for Emu.

"Emu! Food! Here, Emu, Emu, Emu!"

He wasn't anywhere.

I looked at my watch. Ten minutes to five.

"Emu!" I screamed. "Porridge, Emu! Porridge and honey!" Emu loved porridge and honey, but he didn't appear.

I went back inside. I was doing some more quick thinking, trying to make a story up about how the illawarry cassary had escaped.

Maybe I could pull the frozen lamb out of the freezer, cover it in Mum's feather boa and lie it in the middle of the road? A roadkill illawarry cassary.

Where is it?

I made a move towards the freezer, but there was a knock at the door.

It was followed quickly by another knock. Then another. Three knocks — Angus, Martin and Alex. I gulped. Perhaps I could hide under the kitchen table?

"Hey, Flake! I can see you." Angus was tall enough to see through the pane of frosted glass in the door (one of Dad's favourite finds).

He would've also seen the empty driveway so he knew there was no one else here to save me.

"Let us in."

I opened the door and let them in. They crowded around in the hall and I tried to look cool. "Do you want some biscuits? Do you want to play on the computer? I've just got a new game." This wasn't true, but they wouldn't know.

Martin looked interested but Angus shook his head. "We've come to see the illa-whatsit."

"It's an illawarry cassary," I mumbled.

I was just about to launch into 'It's been missing all day' when a screeching, high-pitched squawk came from out the back.

I took no notice, except to think, "Oh, he's back."

But the others jumped.

"What was that?" whispered Alex.

"It sounded pretty mean," said Martin.

The squawk came again, sounding like a murderous howl. Emu must have heard what I said about the porridge. He was on the prowl.

"If that's your bird," said Angus with a glint in his eye, "I want to see it now."

"Well," I began, "now's not really a good time."

Angus elbowed me out of the way and headed towards Dad's workshop. I had no other option but to follow him.

The Illawarry Cassary

Outside the storm was beginning again and storm clouds darkened the sky. We reached the workshop and it was pretty dark.

I switched on Dad's reading lamp and a powerful beam reflected off the mirrors, making everything brighter than daylight.

There was Emu, standing in the doorway, as wet as a fish. His feathers had gone spiky so he looked as if he had some sort of terrible war helmet on.

"Well guys," I said sheepishly, "there's my illawarry cassary."

There was a mighty scream from Martin, who took off as though he'd been bitten by one of his spiders. Then Alex started making gurgling noises in his throat as he walked backwards out of the workshop.

I looked over at Angus and was amazed at his face. He was as white as Mum's tennis socks and I thought I saw his bottom lip trembling.

Emu gave another howl, and just as I was turning around to tell him to clamp his beak shut, Angus bolted after the others. In less than a second, I heard three sets of feet running down the driveway.

I couldn't move. What was going on? Surely they weren't scared of a little wet bantam calling out for his dinner? Hadn't they ever seen a chicken before? I stepped forward to go and get Emu in out of the rain, when I suddenly saw it.

From where Angus, Martin and Alex had stood, Emu was a two-metre-tall, spiky-feathered, war-helmeted, bloodcurdle-screaming, hungry illawarry cassary!

At school these days we never talk about our pets. And no one calls me Flake anymore!

At home I don't complain any more about Dad's mirrors, or the fact that I haven't got a dog. Sometimes I even help Dad polish them and he can't understand why that makes me giggle.

And Emu isn't 'Emu' anymore — that's not a name for an illawarry cassary! I call him Zulu.

I've also started to teach him a thing or two about terriers, just in case the boys ever decide to visit again.

antiques
furniture or other objects from an earlier time

bluffing
pretending, making it up

dandruff
flakes of dry scalp

eyeballed
looked closely at

infectious
germs which are
easily caught

option
choice

reflected
showed an image

rottweiller
a very large breed of dog

specialises
to be an expert in

Pam Harvey

What is your favourite thing?

I have a silver bracelet that is made out of two spoons welded together. I wear that bracelet everywhere and it's left a dent in my arm.

What do you like about yourself?

I like the way I smile a lot, even when things aren't very funny.

Why did the cow jump over the moon?

Because she had very long legs with lots of stringy ligaments in them like kangaroos have. Does this make her a cowaroo?

What is your best midnight snack?

At midnight, the house is very quiet so I have to eat something that doesn't crunch or I'd wake everyone. I eat dried quince and sultanas.

Greg Gaul

What is your favourite thing?

My family and friends.

What do you like about yourself?

I like telling bad jokes.

Why did the cow jump over the moon?

To get to the udder side.

What is your best midnight snack?

Cold curry on toast and a big glass of milk. But then I wake up at 4 am with indigestion and the only thing on telly is ads for exercise machines.